For every parent
and their worried worrier.

Written and Illustrated by
Christopher Fequiere
(fake-ee-air)

Edited by
Dara Fequiere

Oh No, it's back again,
Today is not my day!

It has returned to block my path,
My **Worried Worrier** is in the way.

"We're going to be late," it says.
"Did we miss the bus?"
"I think we're going to be late today!"
My Worriers make such a fuss.

On the bus, choosing where to sit
Should be an easy task.

But when a Worrier is in your seat,
It becomes an **UN**easy ask.

Off the bus, to the playground I go,
For a game of tag before class.

My Worriers continue to pester me,
"What if **we** are chosen last?"

After tag, I head to class,
Where my Worriers stop me in my tracks.
They do not want me to participate,
They do not want me to act.

My Worriers say,
"What if we answer a question,
and the teacher says we are wrong?
The kids in class will laugh at us,
They will make fun of us all day long."

"We should not participate,"
My Worriers start to cry.
"We should not participate,
We should not even **try.**"

On the bus,
I found a place to sit,
And at the playground,
Even though I was chosen last,
I ran, I laughed and made new friends,
Playing tag was such a blast,

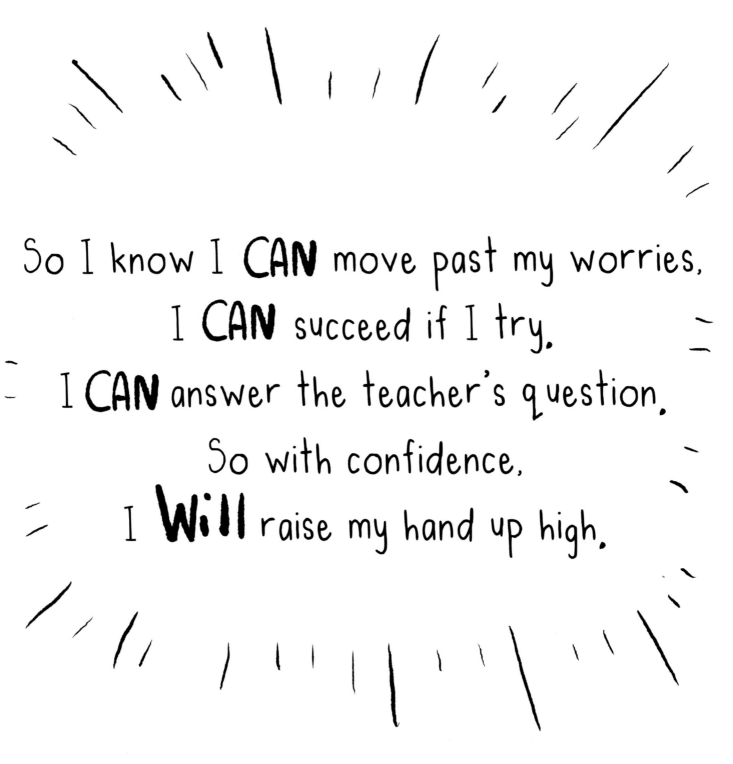

So I know I **CAN** move past my worries,
I **CAN** succeed if I try.
I **CAN** answer the teacher's question,
So with confidence,
I **Will** raise my hand up high.

About the Authors

Author coAuthor

Chris Fequiere is an Illustrator/Animator who has helped create series for DC Comics, Netflix and other global brands. Born and raised in Coney Island, Brooklyn, Chris loves animation, tacos and movie nights with his ~~son~~ Co-Author Oliver and his wife Dara. They still reside in Brooklyn and Chris currently teaches animation at the Borough of Manhattan Community College (BMCC).

Books by Chris Fequiere

purchase at
www. allmyemotions.com

My Worried Worrier   My Tiny Temper

ALL MY EM😠TIONS©

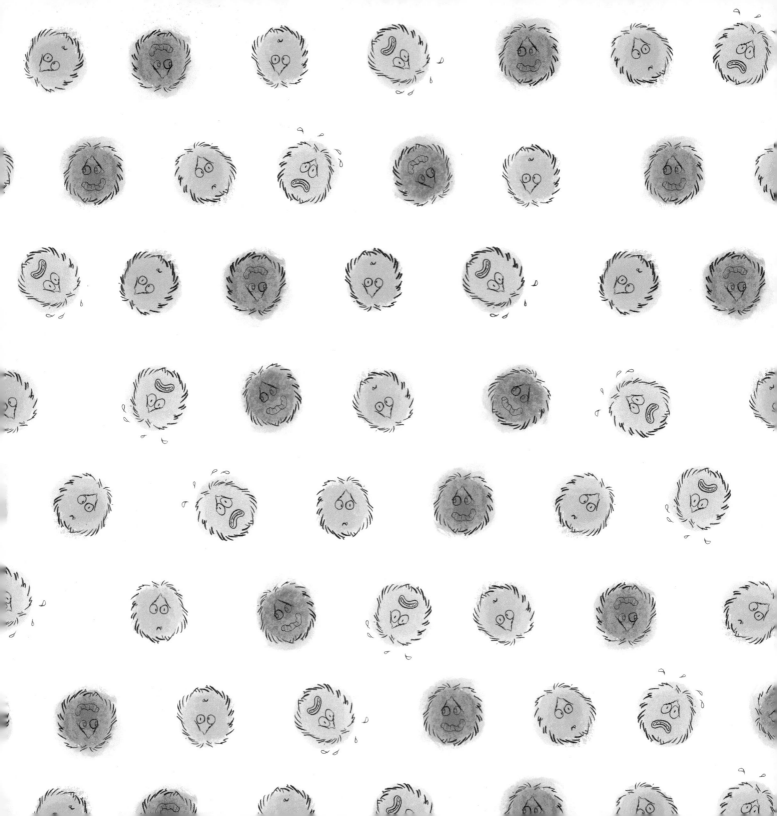